You're Worth MELTING For

By Megan Roth

Illustrated by the Disney Storybook Art Team

Random House 🏠 New York

rhcbooks.com
ISBN 978-0-7364-4081-3
MANUFACTURED IN CHINA
10 9 8 7 6 5 4 3 2 1

Olaf found Elsa and Anna sitting under a tree.

"What are you doing?" he asked.

"We just had the most perfect sister day together," Anna said.

"Because you love each other?" Olaf asked.

"Yes," Elsa said, smiling.

"Aww, that's great!" he exclaimed. "But wait . . . how do you know?"

Elsa turned to Anna and said,

When I'm feeling sad,

you're the person I most want to talk *to.*

You're smart and
adventurous,

always reading *and exploring.*

And you definitely know how to
have fun!

Even when things seem
dark and scary,
you can find
the light.

You always suggest we have

dessert *before dinner.*

And you find different ways each day to make me *smile.*

You're my little sister and my best friend.

Anna was next.
Ever since we were kids,

I've always known how much you *care.*

You amaze me with
your kindness,
your generosity,
and your spirit.

You're **always there** to lend a hand

to *anyone* who needs it.

You're creative
and hardworking,

and you **never give up.**

You know the best games!

You use your *magic* to make

the world better.

I can always count on you to explore new places,

and to be the *best sister* I could ask for.

"And I love you," Anna finished.
"I love you, too," Elsa said, smiling.
"You're *both* worth melting for!"
Olaf cheered.